GRANDMA'S CHRISTMAS SURPRISE

Alison Grunwald

Illustration by Mike Phillips (Beehive Illustration).

With thanks to literary consultant Claire Wingfield for her
invaluable help (www.clairewingfield.co.uk).

Published by Blue Robin Press.

*Robins are loved for their beauty, speed and bravery. They
are also rather cunning and will dart in to steal a meal from
a much larger bird when it is not looking! They are
mischievous, just like Grandma in these stories, and they
can't resist having a bit of fun.*

*We wondered what disguise a robin might use if it did
not want to be noticed, and the answer seemed obvious:
it would mix up some blue poster paint and jump right
in. Who would recognise a blue robin?*

Imagine what naughty tricks it could get up to!

For Polly with all my love, Grandma

WHATEVER NEXT, GRANDMA!

CONTENTS

1

WHAT'S THAT NOISE?

One snowy winter's night, Grandma couldn't sleep. She had thought carefully about her nightclothes, which was why she was wearing her best red-striped pyjamas, a glittery red-and-white hairnet and her favourite tartan bed-socks.

Something made her sit bolt-upright and listen. It was a sound, and she couldn't work out what sort of sound it was.

"Did you hear that noise, Gertrude?" she asked her black-and-white cat, who was snoring contentedly in her basket.

"Miaow," replied Gertrude, grumpily. She had been dreaming and wasn't pleased at being woken up.

"There it is again! Did you hear it?" Grandma hissed.

Gertrude *had* heard it this time, but pretended that she hadn't.

"Well, I'm going to investigate," announced Grandma, slipping her feet into her best orange cowboy boots and admiring herself in the bedroom mirror.

Grandma heard the strange noise again as she crept quietly down the stairs into her cosy sitting-room. She looked around cautiously.

At first, nothing seemed out of place. The room was just as she had left it an hour ago, her empty hot-chocolate mug still waiting to be cleared away from the coffee table and her knitting where she had dropped it, over the back of the sofa.

A loud scraping noise suddenly came from the fireplace and Grandma swung round, just in time to see a large gentleman appear from the chimney in a cloud of dust.

3

He landed on his bottom right in the middle of the hearth and coughed loudly before getting shakily to his feet and brushing himself down.

Grandma just had time to notice a very odd thing: the strange visitor was dressed in the same colours as she was ... red tunic and a red-and-white hat, except *his* hat was pointy, with a white pom-pom on the top, and hers was glittery. His boots were black, whereas hers had stars on them. He had a thick white beard and moustache, and was depositing a lumpy-looking sack against the wall.

2

WHO ARE YOU?

"Who are *you*?" demanded Grandma in her bossiest voice. "What are you doing in my sitting room?"

The portly gentleman smiled and looked rather embarrassed. He clearly had something on his mind.

"Come outside, Madam," he said politely. "It's easier to explain. Oh and you had better put on a coat. It's cold out there!"

Gertrude chose this moment to appear. She had a hunch she knew who the unexpected visitor was and, if she was right, this was one adventure she didn't want to miss.

Grandma was amazed at the sight that met her eyes outside in her small back garden.

"This man must be a dreadful thief," she thought to herself. Not only did he have a sack full of stolen property, but he had clearly taken somebody's sleigh and five brown horses! She ought to let the police know about this straight away.

Then another thought occurred to her.

Were they horses? They looked a bit odd. *Did* horses have antlers?

"What's going on?" she asked, looking sternly at the gentleman in the red hat. "Where did you steal all these horses from?"

Gertrude's ears were pricked like pine cones; she was listening very carefully.

3

WAKE UP, GRANDMA!

"Madam, you don't understand,"
began the beaming gentleman,
patiently. "Do you know what the date
is today?"

"The date?" repeated Grandma,
baffled. "What has the date got to do
with it?"

Gertrude was trying her best to
help Grandma understand, but, as
she couldn't speak, all Grandma
heard, as usual, was a loud
"MIAOW."

"I'll give you a clue," continued the

man, still smiling kindly. "Who lives at the North Pole?"

"Penguins?" replied Grandma, uncertainly.

"Try again. Here's another clue: who delivers presents to all the children every Christmas?"

"The postman, of course," declared Grandma, decisively.

"Right ... in that case, Madam, there's only one thing for it," said the rotund gentleman. "Hop up on the sleigh. We're going for a ride – the fresh air may help you to work out who I am."

Grandma was too baffled to argue and she soon found herself seated comfortably on the sleigh, Gertrude balanced on her lap, with a heavy, warm blanket placed over them by their mysterious visitor.

"PRANCER, AWAY!" instructed the gentleman, firmly.

11

"Ho, ho, ho," he chortled as the sleigh lifted into the night air, the sound of bells drifting magically on the breeze.

Gertrude was thrilled by the sight of hundreds of stars shimmering above them, like diamonds.

"I'm dreaming," thought Grandma, feeling some jokes bubbling to the surface. This often happened in times of peril and, as usual, she couldn't resist trying them out.

Gertrude knew what was coming. "Oh no," she miaowed. "Here we go again."

"What says 'oh, oh, oh'?" Grandma asked the man driving the sleigh.

"Santa walking backwards," quipped the driver in answer to Grandma's question.

"Gosh, that was a lucky guess," thought Grandma, feeling just a bit disappointed.

Another joke swiftly presented itself ...

"What's red and white and red and white and red and white?" she asked. He wouldn't know *this* one.

"Santa rolling down a hill!" chortled the bearded gentleman. These jokes were obviously easy for him.

"How *does* he know the answers?" wondered Grandma. "Bet this one will catch him out!"

"What do you call a cat in the desert?" she asked.

"Oh that's an old one ... Sandy Claus," replied the man, smiling.

"MIAOW," yelled Gertrude. "Wake up, Grandma!"

A startling idea suddenly occurred to Grandma, who glanced down for the first time, her eyes widening in surprise as snowflakes landed on her eyelashes. They were flying high above the earth.

"My goodness," she cried, the puzzle suddenly unravelling. "It's Christmas Eve, isn't it?"

"Yes, it is," agreed the man in the red suit, his silver buttons sparkling in the moonlight.

"And those *aren't* horses, are they?" she gasped, suddenly understanding.

"No they aren't," replied the man, grinning happily.

"They're *reindeer*!" Grandma whispered to herself, as the realization finally dawned on her. "You're Father Christmas, aren't you?" she cried, at last. The penny had finally dropped!

"Yes, Madam, I am," said Santa Claus, a broad smile on his jolly, round, face. "And a very merry Christmas to you both!"

4

GRANDMA'S BRILLIANT IDEA

Grandma pinched herself on the arm, just to check she wasn't dreaming. Then she looked down again at the villages flashing past, far below. She could just make out smoke curling from chimneys and bright colours twinkling from hundreds of Christmas trees and fairy lights.

"Good heavens, Santa," she gasped, her breath billowing into the cold night. "Where's our first stop?"

All night long Santa scrambled nimbly down chimneys, leaving gifts for all the children. The last cottage, however, presented him with a problem. The chimney was just too narrow.

"I may get stuck," he fretted. "What shall I do? There's a sick little girl inside who has asked for some coloured felt-tip pens, so she can draw her mother some pictures. Oh dear!" He looked close to tears.

Grandma stared at Gertrude whilst a brilliant idea began forming in her mind. From Grandma's expression, Gertrude knew something was brewing that she might not like.

"Why don't we send *Gertrude* down the chimney with the little girl's Christmas present instead of you?" Grandma suggested.

Father Christmas clapped his hands. "Yes, why not!" he beamed. It did seem like an excellent idea. "Gertrude, are you *willing* to be Santa?" he asked the surprised cat. "After all, you've already got the claws!"

"Why *do* I always get involved in Grandma's adventures?" miaowed Gertrude, her fur standing on end. But she knew she would deliver the felt-tips. If not, the little girl would have no present waiting for her on Christmas morning ... she would be so disappointed.

5

GERTRUDE IS VERY BRAVE

Santa popped Gertrude into a soft, red-and-white coat, leaving her tail free for balance, then tied a fine rope around her tummy and lowered her carefully down the chimney. The felt-tip pens, all wrapped up in sparkly paper, dangled from a red ribbon clipped to the rope.

Down went the cat, her green eyes squeezed shut until she felt her paws landing on wooden logs. Opening her eyes, she scampered swiftly away from the fireplace towards a shimmering silver Christmas tree. In a trice she had popped open the clip, and, using her little pink nose, deftly pushed the present underneath the tree.

Just in time, because suddenly she felt herself being hoisted gently back towards the chimney.

Up and up she floated, as Santa skilfully wound the rope into a ball until Gertrude was safely installed on

Grandma's lap again.

"*I did it*!" she miaowed excitedly, and, for once, Grandma understood and stroked her lovingly.

"That was wonderful, Gertrude. You are a very brave little Santa Claws. We thank you!" beamed Santa, feeing happy again. The five reindeer didn't want to be left out and snorted in unison, shaking their heads and ringing their bells loudly!

6

SANTA'S LAST SURPRISE

Father Christmas swung the glittering sleigh around, urging the animals to gallop even faster through the twinkly night sky.

Their final stop before daybreak was Grandma's own snowy back garden, where Santa politely helped her, and Gertrude, climb down from the sleigh. Grandma folded the cosy blanket neatly and handed it to Santa, along with the little coat that Gertrude had borrowed.

25

"It was so nice to meet you, at last," she smiled. "You see, I wasn't *quite* sure you were real before tonight," she added, bashfully.

"Not real! How amusing," chortled Santa, his cheeks growing even more rosy. "Just take a look under your Christmas tree when you get in. Merry Christmas, ho, ho, ho!"

And before Grandma could say 'mince pies' Santa's sleigh had lifted off into the starry sky and was lost from sight, the sound of the reindeers' tinkling bells growing fainter and fainter.

Grandma and Gertrude hurried back inside the cottage and were thrilled at what they saw!

"How did he do that?" murmured Grandma, staring at two new presents neatly covered in colourful paper, waiting to be unwrapped, under her little Christmas tree.

"Well he *is* Father Christmas," miaowed Gertrude to her friend.

"He *really* is," echoed my Grandma. "Well, well,well!"

NOW TEST YOUR MEMORY!

1. What makes Grandma sit bolt-upright in bed at the beginning of the story?

2. How does Grandma's gentleman visitor arrive in her sitting room?

3. Grandma and the visitor are wearing clothes of the same colour, but something looks different. Can you remember what it is?

4. What day is it in the story?

5. What kind of animals has Grandma mistaken for horses? How does she realise her mistake?

6. Who is the man driving the sleigh?

7. Why doesn't Santa go down the chimney of the last cottage?

8. Who goes down the chimney instead of Santa?

9. What present does Gertrude deliver to the little girl in the cottage?

10. What is the surprise waiting for Grandma and Gertrude when they return home from their adventure?

Gertrude says look in the story to see if you're right!

Would you like to write a story about Grandma and Gertrude? Here are a few ideas to get you going!

❄ Decide who and what the tale is about.

❄ Find a comfortable place to write or type.

❄ Build your story with plenty of interest.

❄ Use great descriptions of your characters and setting.

❄ Remember to end your tale as well as it started. We all love a good ending!

Watch out for

Grandma's
Jungle
Adventure

**Coming
Soon!**

ABOUT THE AUTHOR

A Londoner, Alison Grunwald has always loved writing comic stories and poems for children. She enjoyed working in primary schools teaching early reading to children arriving from other countries. One of the ways she did this was by inventing and singing a rap which made them laugh and helped them learn vowel sounds!

Alison has been a radio and news-paper reporter and a doula. This is someone who looks after mums when they are expecting a baby and helps them learn how to feed and look after it. Sometimes twins arrive and Alison knows what to do because she has twins herself!

These days Alison has lots of grand-children who help her with suggestions for her funny stories.

You can get in touch with Alison at: a.grunwald@btinternet.com to send your stories, jokes or just to say hello. (Please get permission from a grown-up before sending your email.)

If you enjoyed this book, please look out for more of Grandma and Gertrude's adventures, and please help to spread the word by telling your friends, teachers, cousins and grandmas. You might even like to write a book review and send it to Alison. She would love to hear from you – but for now, it's until the next time from Alison, Grandma and Gertrude!

ALSO BY ALISON GRUNWALD

ISBN: 978-1-83802-940-1

Merry Christmas
to you all!

Made in the USA
Columbia, SC
07 December 2020